JAMES P WHITE

The World Within
A Novella

Xii Press
1st Edition

Dedication:
For My Grandson James Pacey White

The World Within

When he woke up that morning he had decided to live one day of his life, today, outside of reality. He would step out of it just as every morning the twenty-four hours before had changed from present to past. These twenty-four hours would cut to the bone. He would learn he thought what reality really was if he could get away from the learned reality he knew.

He stretched out his arms and drew in a clean, refreshing breath. He blew it out forcefully.

He got out of bed and went into the large bathroom. He tried not to name the face he saw in the mirror. Don't tell yourself who you are, he thought. He splashed water onto his face and looked again. Did living reality mean he didn't have a past that told him who he was?

I am myself, he thought. The one that no one told me to be.

He left the bathroom quickly, leaving the towel he used to dry his cheeks, on the floor. Outside the windows, the cloudy sky blocked the view of the high-rises nearby.

He sat a moment on the foot of the bed, deciding how to go about the day. Then he dismissed the thought. It would be easier to let reality come to him, rather than seek it out. He dressed for the cold he could see through the windows. I am here, he thought, come get me. He meant, get me out.

As he rode the elevator downstairs, he could sense everything about the other two people around him. It wasn't about what they wore or who they appeared. He sensed their standing beside him, like objects placed on a conveyer. His first impulse was to step back. He did. A second later, he opened his mouth and he screamed. It was a huge bellow that shook the other two. As he looked at them, they trembled. He kept his lips tight. He looked directly into their eyes. No one spoke. When the elevator doors opened, they hurried out.

He took his time. The scream was something he had just discovered. He walked confidently out of the elevator and across the entryway and through the glass doors.

The traffic was nothing to him. The sidewalk was hard and stretched ahead. The sky was cut off by the buildings. Did something need to tell him where he go? He asked. Yes. He felt the hunger in his stomach. And he felt more, a need to explore. To see. To begin again. He realized that what was important was what he believed. He would believe in what he learned for himself.

The echo of learning all his life was like a rope around his neck. It bound him to pathways just like horses with blinders in harness. Forget it, he said to all the learning he had ever had. As he walked, he was freed from it, all of it. I'm telling myself what reality is today, he thought. The word today frightened him, but he couldn't get rid of it. He wasn't crazy. He just wanted to see, to find out for himself. Did he believe in God? He looked up at the sky. Yes, he had more belief this moment than any other in his life. But it was not the learned God. It was something that made him honor himself and everything around him that he was about to perceive.

He stopped at a red light, then told himself never to look at them again. Instead, he noticed the woman standing beside him. She mattered, as if he had never seen a woman before. Her clothing was strange and bright, and her hair, cut short, showed under her knit cap. She smiled at him. He looked directly into her eyes and for a second, she stared back. Then she hurried away. It was the first person he had ever seen at a crosswalk. Their meeting of the eyes went beyond everything he assumed of others usually.

I will look at everyone, he told himself. Look at them so that they feel compelled to look back at me. He knew he would meet someone he was supposed to.

There was already something foretold about what he was doing. He sensed it. The meaning of life was in a reality he was about to discover for himself. It made him tremble. As he walked behind the woman whose eyes he had met, he realized that she was not someone he should speak to. Everything about her day, her week, her year, was already planned. She was an emblem of civilization.

He passed a shoe store, a clothing store, a jewelry store. The things were less useful to him than a pile of trash would have been. In fact, trash sounded rich because of what it showed.

Without having a need to plan what he was doing, his mind opened up. He thought the words "human activity." This meant work, school, sports, tv, and well defined things. But what was the basis of human activity, he asked himelf. None of those specific things. They only doctored things. He looked up at a small patch of sky. He would have to get out of the city..

Getting away from the reality he knew was more difficult because he knew of its conveniences. He had hoped to get beyond this, so he told himself that he would have to walk wherever he went.

A cold breeze blew against his face. It felt very much outside him. And he walked against it, his hands in the pockets of his coat. At the first café he passed, he went inside, sat on a stool at the counter, and ordered black coffee.

"Freezing outside," the counterman said.

He tried to forget what freezing meant, below 32 degrees. A moment later, he sipped the steaming coffee the man brought. He started to say something when he thought about how almost every word he knew had come from organized learning. He nodded, then smiled, and the man smiled back.

He told himself he would smile at everyone he could.

Another man sat beside him and ordered breakfast. He smiled at him. The man, surprised, smiled back. It was comfortable.

The other people in the café were doing what they had been told, having breakfast. He felt something genuine about their eating together. But he knew that after eating most would go their own way, to live their day as they were supposed to. Those who sat together, talked. Most of the others looked at their cell phones, waiting to talk meanwhile. He suddenly stood up. He felt that he had something to say to all of them, not to any one person. No one looked at him until he began to talk. "I just want to say hello," he said.

Several people nodded and even mumbled hello back. He could see that they were embarrassed. But he wasn't. "Anyone want to come with me today?" he asked.

People stirred, like he was crazy. The counterman, frozen, moved into action and began to walk toward him. He smiled at the counterman who hesitated, then smiled back.

After paying, he left the café and walked slowly, his coat buttoned up.

"Excuse me," he heard and turned around. The woman was younger than he and still putting on her coat. She wore a knit cap, too.

He stopped for her.

"Why did you do that?" she asked. "Why did you talk to everybody?"

"Well, I didn't know anyone," he said.

"Why did you say anything?"

"Why are you saying anything?" he asked.

"I agree," she said. "I think it was wonderful."

"And I think your talking is wonderful."

She returned the look directly into the eyes. "Do you need something?" she asked.

"Yes," he said. "I need everything."

For a second neither spoke. He waited for her because he had spoken honestly.

"Are you OK?"

"I'm not sure what that means," he said.

She laughed suddenly. "I don't either."

"Okay is not a state," he said.

"I just meant do you need anything."

"I told you," he said.

She smiled, then bit her lip. "Thank you for telling me hello," she said.

"Hello," he said. "Hello again."

"Hello," she said. Both of them laughed.

"Where are you going?" she asked. "I've got to get to work."

He said nothing. She touched his hand, then turned around and hurried down the street.

Going to work, he thought, wondering for a moment where that idea had come from. Going to work. He started back down the street. He seemed to be headed for the river.

The cold didn't let up as he walked faster. Closer to the river, the wind increased and the sky was more grey. He could feel it blow against his coattails.

He asked himself if he had found any reality in his day so far. He thought yes, he had.

Am I like a homeless person he asked himself. Is that what individual reality is? He knew it wasn't. He had not abdicated from society. He was exploring something he was well aware of, to see if he could understand what his daily life really meant. So much of life was mental. Didn't Alzheimer's and suicide show that? In Alzheimer's a life is disturbed maybe totally and in the other, life as we know it is ended. Should life be lived without an awareness of what reality really is? He didn't think so. Or, if life as he knew it was totally learned, then he wanted to know that, too. So what he was trying to do was to live in a way he wouldn't have considered normal, learned. But he didn't mean insanity or withdrawal.

True, he was ignoring his friends and relatives. But their voices were part of what he was getting away from.

At the river, he watched the waves like others there, did. Light was bright on the water even though the sky was grey. Tugboats were passing. In the distance was a ship, going somewhere. My body is my ship, he thought. It has a destination. All I've done so far is not to go to work this morning.

He sat on the bank and listened to the tugs. Somehow everything he had learned made him want to cry. He didn't know why. Even the sound of the tug and the feel of the vibration on it when he had experienced that, made him sad. Memory made him sad. This is a part of reality, he thought. My memory makes me sad. Even the good memories make me sad because they are gone. That is not what I have learned. That is real. Even the memory of this morning makes me sad. I should have said more to the people in the café. And my feeling that I should have done something is part of my reality. It is not what I learned; it is what I feel.

My feelings are a deep part of my reality. I cannot think about that now.

He got up and began to walk toward the small park above the river. There were many people there.

His sadness came from the beauty of the morning, too. The hot coffee, the woman who cared about him, the movement of the water, the sound of the tug, the beauty soaked into his mind and his heart and made him feel that he was not just this body walking, but something more, hearing more, feeling more, doing more. And he thought that this was part of why he believed in God. He could never feel this on his own. His thoughts and feelings that took him far from his body came from something deeper and more important in life than he was.

He did not feel important at all as he walked. And that was preferred. Importance, he thought, is not important.

He regretted screaming at the people on the elevator. He had no idea now why he had done it.

How can you do anything without using what you've learned from others, he asked himself.

He was determined to find out.

At the park he began to think about his heart and what it meant. He felt it because it was like the view of the river. He didn't think about what his heart had experienced. It was about how strong and beautiful his heart was. He knew his heart had tentacles and rays. It was in every part of his body, especially his eyes when he looked up at the sky. There was a place in his heart that could open up and give him—give everyone—everything that he was. He closed his eyes and felt grateful to his heart for being what it was, what it had been. Thank you my heart he thought. And he felt love for this part of his body. He felt the same love that came from it.

There were a lot of limitless things about him, he knew. His mind wasn't one of them. It was walled in by learning. But his heart, his eyes, his sense of touch, his hearing, his senses were only limited in themselves—the things they brought into him were the limitless things, the beautiful sounds, the harsh ones, the satin touch, the sunset, the stars, the footprints that all these had made, each of these had made, were his reality. Forever.

He stood up and took a deep breath. Then he began walking again.

I must do something he told himself. My reality is not to do nothing. I must do something. It didn't seem to matter what it was as long as it was something he felt he should do. There was the should again.

What should I do? he asked.

He decided to pick up trash from the street. It seemed useful and interesting. First, what was the trash and how did it get on the street? He took a used paper cup with red lipstick on the rim. He wondered what the woman had been talking about when she drank from it. There were several fries no one had eaten. A wrinkled wrapper from a fast food place, printed with the name of the place. It belonged to that fast food place more than to the woman who had left it. And why had she been in such a hurry?

It is my reality to know and imagine things about other people, he thought. This is not learned. Maybe what I think about them is learned, but my imagining and knowing is essential to who I am. I cannot live without understanding that there are other people like me. Was this true? he asked himself. Yes.

It didn't bother him that what he picked up was not clean. Next was a straw, then an old purse that was empty and left in a doorway. He could tell it had been used a long time. But who had thrown it away there? He left a pair of underwear on the sidewalk, then picked up a ball point pin. It worked. Another paper cup and something entirely different, a nickel someone had dropped. He took the trash to a bin at the corner and put the nickel back on the street for someone to have. He didn't want to deal with money today.

He began to view himself as animals who had no organized learning, but he couldn't think of any. Didn't all animals learn from their families and others? Did snakes? He didn't want to be like a snake anyway. Were cows lounging around under trees or eating grass for hours doing what they were taught to do? He thought of the number of insects and animals he'd encountered and never read about. About trees he had no idea of their nomenclature. About rocks he didn't study in geology. About things he'd learned on his own, mostly when he was a kid. That learning was different. It wasn't being told what to think but it was telling yourself what to recognize.

He realized that in order to find a reality on his own he had to think about what he had learned on his own. He thought that it was many many things. Most of it had to do with how he felt. It was harder for people to tell you how to feel than to feel things on your own outside of what they said.

He wondered for a moment if when he died, he got a chance to be himself more.

He wondered what his language would be like if he hadn't learned it at home and in school. It had to be based on sounds he could make. He supposed some of the sounds would mimic those he learned. What would it be like for him to have his own language and what on earth would that language be like? A dog's growling, an elephant's shrill, a turkey's gobble, a cat's meow, an alligator's hissing, a moose's bellow, and endlessly on and on. What was the basic human sound outside of learned language? He opened his mouth, felt his tongue and saliva and made the sound 'oh'. It seed perfectly natural. 'Oh." He liked it a lot, with a high tone He tried saying it lower. Unnatural. He hummed a moment. Yes, that was natural. But so many words, like "hypochondriac," were idiotic to say. Or try "Pithecanthropus Erectus," so absurd. All the terms and learned words struck him as dumb. "Historiography," for instance. Or "id". His mind was filled with words that were not natural. He decided to make up his own sentence with his own sounds and listen to it. He tried "Oh" and "Ah" and "Brr" and "K" and others. Finally he came up with, "Kerr Ahhh Ohh Tee." He accentuated the "Ohh". He liked it very much. How much better it would have been he thought if everyone had at least a smidgen of a right to make up his own language. Other than babies.

He decided to try speaking his own sounds to the person he saw sitting in the doorway of the next building he passed. He was reading a newspaper. He smiled and the person in the doorway smiled back. Then he looked at the man directly in the eye and said, "Kerr Ahh Ohh Tee." He followed this up with, "Waa Waa Puu Tee." The man looked puzzled then laughed. "Yee ko," he said, laughing, and he laughed, too. "Ta Ta Mmm," he said. The man laughed, then shook his head. "I'm busy," he said and looked back at the newspaper.

He walked on, feeling rather good at the outcome. Now what if we made up words that had meaning? he thought. Was that where language came from? Of course. But how lucky those first people were who just sputtered what came naturally and didn't have to learn a lot of garbage. Yes, many words had come to mean garbage, he thought. Not just curse words. Words like "exam," "test," "failed," "jail," "prison," etc. He would take those words and many others out of the human vocabulary because they misled others.

He felt better, walking on. He wiped his hands on his pants and decided to think about what else he had learned that he would take out of his head. Much of it was garbage that taught him to judge others. Were they smart or beautiful or rich or important or known or were they of a certain color or spoke a certain way or lived a certain way. What on earth was all of that? Get rid of it.

He wondered what it would be like to get rid of everything in his life that had made him feel superior? The best grades, the most complimentary remarks, the bonuses, the promotions, the invitations. Toss them out. Did he feel like everyone else? Did everyone feel like everyone or did everyone feel different? Wasn't it natural to feel different? He thought it was, even when everyone was alike. What on earth did that imply? Were people afraid of being people, of being like everyone else? Well, they were. He was, too.

He saw a woman just passing him. "Thank you for picking up the trash," she said.

She was very thin, with a wrinkled face and a thin

smile. Her voice was kind.

"I'm supposed to do it," he said.

"We all are," she said, "but not many of us do. Just look at how much litter people throw on the sidewalk."

He nodded.

"I live nearby. I appreciate what you are doing."

He nodded.

"I've never seen you before."

"I've never seen you before," he said.

"I hope I see you again," she said, passing by. She gave him a broad smile as she left.

Somehow it made him not want to pick up any more trash. He was doing it for himself.

The thought crossed his mind that many of the people in the café he had said hello to, wouldn't want to see him again. Perhaps this was what he was feeling. A kind of incongruous reaction to someone's being nice when you don't know them. I'm wrong, he said. And he wished he had said something kind and even loving to the woman. When he thought about her smile now he realized her thought was beautiful. He wanted his to be.

Isn't it natural to want to be beautiful in how you look at others? he thought. Doesn't it make you feel better? He determined that throughout the entire day he was going to be kind and complimentary to everyone he met. No matter who they were. It was about him, not them. And he vaguely thought this was what he had learned in the Bible. But that was okay. He couldn't just toss out everything he had learned, could he?

If he wasn't going to pick up trash he had to think of something else to do. Maybe it shouldn't be so helpful. And he didn't like getting his hands so dirty. He decided that he would look for old people who needed help and give them a hand. It was hard to be old and frail. He would be someday.

But no one like that was in front of him so he just

walked along, enjoying thinking on his own, finding his own reality. It was, after all, mental wasn't it? And he was kind of thinking outside of what he had learned, as much as he could at the moment. He somewhat thought that he was seeing something of his nature that he hadn't known before, but he didn't know how to articulate it. So he didn't try.

He never thought about his own death. Sometimes if he was sad, he did, wondering how others would feel if he were gone. But he almost never did this. Death was in the news and very popular. It was in films and TV and in books and in the cemetery. It was in funeral homes. But it was a topic for old people. Is it natural for me to think about death? he thought. Well, if he hadn't been so busy learning and at work, he probably would think about death every day. And thinking about it would make him rethink his life. His own reality should include his awareness that he was alive because he was going to die. He wasn't alive so he could just enjoy himself; he was also alive because he was going to die. That was the part he didn't think about. And if he did think about it, he realized that how he lived his life was more important than how he enjoyed what he was doing at the moment. Even the old people who he knew, his grandmother for instance, thought more about her clothes than about dying. The problem was that no one knew what was death was and the various theories were just that.

Do I expect anything? he asked himself. It wasn't in nature he thought, to "expect." Did cows expect? Should he? And if he didn't, how would that affect how he felt. Maybe it was a good thing because he wouldn't worry so much. Lately he had begun to worry a lot. Was it because he expected something bad to happen or he expected something would interfere with something good happening? Was expectation learned? Of course he expected a peach to taste like a peach. But this was different. He couldn't expect anything all day.

And while he was at it, why didn't he do what his nature wanted him to do? Just luxuriate in every single moment. He asked himself: have I been happy this morning? He had. So, why? He couldn't answer. He never could have imagined himself picking up trash on the wharf along the river or screaming on the elevator or telling an entire café hello. Why had that made him happy? It had.

He wanted to whistle. He felt wonderful at the moment because he was going to do exactly what he wanted. That mattered, his decision to do just that. How much of his life was bothered with doing what others wanted? Too much for sure. And when he did that, didn't he usually just get judged for doing it? All of this, he thought, looking not just at his thoughts, but at the wharf, the apartments, the street, the cars, all of this is mine in my head because I am free. I do not have to own it for it to be mine. I own it because it is in my life. I own everything in my life. The next thing I know about my reality is that what is in my life matters. I need to look closely at what comes in because when it's there, I own it. Thank you, God, he said to himself. Thank you because I have that decision. Only you could give it to me. And only I can decide.

I will make decisions that I am willing to take responsibility for. I will not make decisions for others, which is their responsibility, he thought.

And if I leave my mind totally blank at this moment, he thought, what comes into it next? There was nothing immediately. It felt wonderful.

But all of this current of thought, all of this endless asking and evaluating and all of this giving and taking, what did it mean in his life? Did each individual item have meaning? it couldn't. It was like watching a movie and seeing each individual moment of the editing. He wished God would do the editing and he could do the seamlessly living. Because living wasn't easy even though it was delightful and it was delightful, all of it even the undelightful parts. It was like life/death. it was like getting pinched and not pinched at the same time. He felt very grateful for it and tremendously confused.

He hurt for those who committed suicide and could not take what happened to them. He could not judge them, but he hurt for them because he thought that no matter how horrible something was, there was something wonderful to take its place, even if it meant accepting the horrible. There was just no way to take the value of life itself. The only way to do that was to judge yourself rather than let God judge you. God would never have told those people to commit suicide or have killed them. If he had wanted to kill them he could have. God wanted them to see, to come back to where they should be in the first place, outside of the difficulties of experiences, to the underlying love in the world. That love is a world bank for every single person who is unhappy.

And while he was at it, he thought that the only reason those people in that café were upset at his talking was because they loved him. Otherwise they would not have cared if he was crazy. He had to remember, in his real world, not to frighten others who lived just as he did. They were in the world together, like flowers on trees. There was no need to threaten anyone.

Again, he regretted the elevator.

I'm hungry he told himself because his stomach told him so. There was a place he knew that had great shrimp but since he knew it he couldn't go there. He had to go to a new place. And he did. He walked along until suddenly he smelled something so good, that he just opened the door to the café, walked in and sat down at a table, his stomach growling with pleasure.

He ordered the shrimp like everyone around him did. Maybe he'd found an even better place.

He had to ask himself when the food came if it

was all right for him to eat another animal. He threw
away the name for it. He wasn't eating shrimp he was
eating animal like himself. It smelled wonderful. Would
you eat it if it were another person? he asked. He had to
think about it. It wasn't natural for a cow to eat a cow
etc. So he wouldn't eat a human finger no matter how
good it smelled. But how did the shrimp get onto the
plate in front of him? And did vegetables not have any
feeling? What did shrimp eat? Did that matter? Well, it
kind of did. If the shrimp ate life, which it did, then why
couldn't he eat the shrimp? He could. It was just part
of life's eating life, or like the getting pinched and then
not pinched. What he was eating was no longer getting
pinched. And what if he were fried and on the plate?
Would that be okay? Not being suicidal, he thought it
would because something was going to eat him anyway
even if it was after he was dead and rotting in the coffin.
And why let it go to waste? So dig in, he told himself.
And he did.
     He reminded himself to come back and eat it
again, too. Best shrimp he had ever had.
     As he walked down the block, he saw a woman
carrying her bags of groceries to her apartment. She sat
them down and one spilled. She looked up at him.
     He was irritated she wanted him to help her, but
he was going to do it. He placed the spilled groceries
in the bag. She lifted the bags and opened the door. She
thanked him and went inside.
     He felt better event though he had resisted. In fact,
he wondered what her apartment was like, but he knew
she wouldn't let him carry the groceries inside. That part
of her was afraid of him. So he went on.
     Actually animals seemed to want others to be
afraid of them for self-protection and dominance. He
felt dominant over the woman because he was stronger.
And he liked that. But he didn't want her to be afraid of
him. Did he want anyone to be afraid of him? He thought

about it for a minute. Well if he were a bull, he would. Or if he were a lion, especially. Or many other things, but he was a human being. Hitler did, he thought. Quit thinking of history, he thought, think of yourself. Do you want others to be afraid of you? He kind of did, to tell the truth. But afraid in a good way. If there were such a thing. He wanted admired. To feel strong. To feel protected and protective. Fear made you and others safe or it made you unsafe. Wouldn't it be better to just get rid of fear altogether? But you had to be afraid of burning yourself or getting into an accident. Fear was one of those things that just had to be taken on face. But no, he didn't really want anyone to be afraid of himself, especially himself. He wondered if suicides were afraid of themselves, when they realized that they could do real harm to themselves.

"Would you like to buy this?" a guy asked. He held up a ring which looked like a gemstone.

"What?"

"You want to buy it? I am selling it cheap."

He was interested in where the guy got the ring. "Do you have others?" he asked.

"Yes, follow me."

He followed him around the corner to the alley. The man took a black bag out of his pocket and opened it. There were several items, a gold chain, earrings, and a bracelet.

"Let me see it," he said.

"Be careful. Don't let anyone see you."

"I'm just looking at it."

"Well, watch it."

He took the gold chain. "Is it real?"

"Of course it's real."

"How much is it?"

"Forty dollars."

"Why is it so cheap? Where did you get it?"

"It doesn't matter where. See the price tags on them?"

"Yes."

"Are they stolen?"

"What?"

"Are they?"

"I'm leaving."

"They aren't real."

"They are real."

"Where did you steal them?"

"I'm out of here." The guy turned and hurried away, down the alley.

He watched him leave. He asked himself if he wanted the stolen jewelry. Yes, he did.

He looked to see if anyone else like a cop was watching. He saw no one and turned back to the street.

Would he like to steal something? He would let himself if it were his reality. What would he steal? The shrimp was the best thing he saw all day. What did he want more of when he was thinking about his own reality? Did he want more things? Another car? Another condo? Another suit? Another gold chain? He didn't need any of it. He didn't need a thing that kept him from realizing who he was. Everything owned him: his job, his bank account, his fiancé, his mother. But not today. Nothing owned him today and he would stay away from things the most he possibly could. Did most animals own things? Did they? Birds? Cows? Turtles? Fish? What did they own? Were they free because they didn't. Maybe they were.

And they stole food from each other. But no one owned the food they stole. They just dominated and pushed the other aside. It wasn't like stealing. It was bullying.

Am I like an animal in nature? he asked? What else could I be? What could I even suppose I could be? Could a bird imagine he's not a bird in nature? Could he think he was a tree? What a dumb bird. Could a bunny imagine he was something else? Everything was part of nature no matter what it thought of itself. And poor caged birds and animals were being ripped from their environments.

Anyway, he had no interest in stealing or hurting anyone else.

He glanced around, but didn't see the guy selling the jewelry.

"Hey, Jim," he heard. His name is Jim

He turned, and there was a friend of his. William, who worked with his company.

"You enjoying a day off?"

"Trying to," he said.

"Me, too. We haven't talked in a while. I heard you got engaged."

"Yes."

"To Susan."

"Yes."

"Well, I've got a new kid on the way."

"Really?"

"So what are you doing here?"

"I'm just taking a day off."

"You want to get a drink?"

He hesitated. Could he talk to him and be himself, not who he was supposed to be? "Why not?"

"Let's go there." He pointed to a bar at the corner.

They walked to the bar, ordered a beer and sat at a small table that overlooked the street.

"What's it like to have kids?" he asked.

"Great."

He nodded. "Great?"

"I'd do anything for my kids."

He nodded. "What's it like?" he asked again.

"They keep you busy. And they cost a lot. But I love them to death. You'll see."

"I hope so. Do you think this is a good place for them to live?"

"In the city?"

"In our way of life."

"Well, it's too busy. They all have lessons. And they have school. And they have cell phones. And computers."

"Like you."

"Essentially. I have work."

"Do you like it?"

"That they have cell phones and computers? Not really. But there's nothing I can do."

"And you have them, too."

"And you do, too."

"Right now I do."

"Don't think about it. You need these things."

He smiled. "Yes."

"What responsibilities do you have as a father?" he asked.

His friend grinned. "About as much as I can handle."

"Like?"

"Like feeding them, getting them in school, paying doctors, clothing them, all that."

"What else?"

"Well, I'm responsible for their well being."

"Okay. What else?"

"What else what else?"

"How do you teach them to deal with their own emotions? How to handle stress, to deal with love and hate and ambition and their desires?"

"I think they have to teach themselves that."

"Do they? You mean let them learn it at school and church and with friends?"

"Well, what else?"

"If you know how to handle yours, shouldn't you teach them that?"

"They are different from me."

"So you can't teach them because they aren't you? But they are part of you."

"What are you getting at?"

"What is reality to your kids? Is it your reality?"

"Yes."

"What is your reality?"

"It's everyone's reality."

"Really? Everyone has a reality? Is that what reality is, what everyone thinks together is reality?"

"Yes."

"So you don't think on your own?"

"I do. But I'm not being silly like you are."

"Then what is your reality?"

"I face my life every day. I live my own life."

"Is it your life?"

"I have no idea," he said. "If it isn't, I don't want to know about it. I'm not sure I have any idea what you are talking about."

"Well, that is what interests me. I want to find my reality outside of everything I've been taught."

"Okay. When you find it, tell me what it is." He laughed. "Or I'll tell you if I find mine."

"Absolutely."

"Let's have another beer and quit talking about this."

"Absolutely," he said.

Later, he said, "You know we've been friends a long time. That's real. I like you. But I know very little about you. When we do something we aren't thinking. We play tennis, we eat with our wives at the restaurant and talk about the kids and our vacations. But we've never talked about what we really think about anything."

His friend sighed, then took a drink of the beer. "So what do you want to talk about?"

"I'm not sure," he said. "What do you think about all day?"

"I think I'm in a hurry like right now," he said. He looked at his watch. "And I don't have time to talk about nothing. Did you look at how the market went up this morning. Now that's something. We can talk about it."

They talked a few more minutes about it, then separated.

As he walked on, he began to talk to himself. "Listen," he said. And he stopped and listened to himself. Wait a minute, he said. Who am I addressing? Who is it that I'm telling to listen? I know it's myself, but if it is, it's another part of myself. I'm telling one part of myself, or one awareness of myself to listen to the other and think about something. There are two parts of this, regardless. So whom am I addressing?

He was appealing to himself, of course. Some self removed from his normal mind. Some self that was evaluating and could listen and tell him what to think about himself. No matter what anyone else ever advised him, didn't he go to this part to decide for himself? Yes. Well, thank you, he told himself. Do a good job that I don't always do. He was aware that sometimes he went against his own advice. Maybe he shouldn't. There was something respectful about that and he suspected that everyone had a guide within themselves that was a sounding board. Was this conscience? No, because it wasn't just about right from wrong. He had asked it questions about love and health and career and fate. So listen, he said again to himself, are you there? Are you awake? Are you listening? He chuckled. Yes, that part was sound as a fiddle and here he was, with it, knowing that it was definitely his friend and for him.

Do animals other than humans do what they really want to do? he asked. Do turtles or rabbits? He supposed cows lucky enough to be in fields enjoyed eating and chewing all day. They had to because they did it. But did rabbits enjoy hopping? He bet they did. He bet that birds loved soaring and with their wonderful eyesight, spying everything below. He didn't want to hop, but he'd love to soar, he thought. And he would like to leap like a deer even if he didn't want to hop. Crawling like a snake would be depressing. Just quivering along. Swimming like a fish, oh yes, that would be delightful. He had been amazed at how fast some swam. He'd seen minnows jumping out of the water up and out and down, and that was exciting, like a race. Yes, they must be racing for the food, he thought. Lions and leopards looked beautiful as they ran.

He stood at another street corner, waiting for a light to change. All of this is in front of you, he thought. Animals soaring, running, walking, hopping, slithering. All of it. The amount of things in his head that came just from his observation, not from what he was told, overwhelmed it. This was what he was looking for. Another part of his reality was that he could look at anyone or anything and see for himself. He could ask this part of himself that seemed to know or to be able to evaluate and pack it away there, while he went on his merry way, pigging up images.

Oh the things he had seen that had brought him pleasure. Snow falling from the sky, water rushing down a creek along rocks under a blue sky with green trees along it, inside a cave with dark and light mirroring light inside. Oh my goodness, his entire world that he saw made him love his eyes as well as his heart. Thank you eyes, he said, and he opened them wide, and took in the building in front of him. He looked at the steel and the glimmering glass and the sunlight flashing against both and at the spire of the building that made him crane his neck to see. Oh thank you eyes, he said. What a joy. What a joy. Why he would never call them eyes. What would he call them? He considered it. He would call them love, and he would call his heart love. Oh my god, he thought, would I call every part of my body love? He would. What else could it be? If he appreciated his heart beating and his eyes seeing, what else could it be? The idea of the rest of his body being part of this, part of what God gave to him, pinged in his head. Oh yes. Oh yes. But he couldn't filter all this idea at once. Later, he said, saving it like a piece of cake to think of later.

This is what I'm talking about when I say reality, he thought. This joy of my thinking. Why couldn't I have told my friend that? Why did I have to dry it down to words that didn't have the joy?

Thoughts are juicy, like watermelons and lemonade, he thought. Thoughts are hard and open like crystals. They shine like diamonds and are black as tar. Oh, the dimensions of thoughts were a clear path in front of him.

He did not control that path. It led him to where he chose to go somewhat and it showed him what it wanted. There was a pathway to his thoughts that was not just his thinking. It was like the steel of the buildings and the clarity of the glass. Just follow me, it beckoned, just trust me to see where I can take you.

Enough, he thought. Enough. Instead, he looked at his feet and watched the boots he wore. Their movement was interesting, too.

Meditation and thinking, he thought, and he dismissed it immediately. Quit thinking what others have told you, he said. Look at the boots for yourself. You aren't finding god there, you are looking at your movement as you walk. It relaxed him, like yawning.

He suddenly heard his cell ring and realized he had left it in his pocket. Instinctively he drew it out.

Susan.

They had broken up a month ago and neither had called. He accepted the call.

"Yes?"

"Honey?"

"You're calling me?"

"I just wanted to know how you are feeling. You were so angry when we talked last."

"Yes, I was."

"I've thought about what I said and I apologize for the way I said it."

"You apologize for telling me you wanted to go our separate ways?"

"No, I apologize for how I told you."

He didn't say anything. The buildings around him turned dark and his boots seemed squashy on the sidewalk. "Yes,"

"I want to be friends with you. I miss your friendship."

He knew that that breakup was part of the reason he had decided to find his own reality. He didn't want to go nuts unhappy and he had to find stability in his life. "Yes," he said

"Quit saying yes."

"You want me to say no?"

"I don't want you to say any particular thing."

"All right," he said, "no."

"What do you mean no?"

"I mean the same thing as when I said yes. I mean yes, no, yes, no."

"You're still hurt."

"Yes, no, yes, no."

Actually the two meant a lot together. He'd never thought of that.

"Honey, can you meet me later? I think we should talk. Someone told me how unhappy you've been."

"Oh."

"Can you meet today?"

"Um hmm," he said. But he wasn't thinking. He was feeling so strong that no thought could enter.

"Great, how about we meet at Tony's in an hour? Are you doing something that you can't get free?"

"An hour is good," he said.

"You know I would never want to hurt you," she said.

He had absolutely no idea what to say.

"I still care about you."

He felt like crying when she said that, like she didn't care for him, not like she had. It was like telling him it was all over again. He said nothing.

"Don't be like that," she said.

"Like what?"

"Quiet."

He sighed.

"What are you doing, anyway?"

"I'm walking."

"Aren't you at work?"

"I don't think so," he said, chuckling. "I walk at work though. But I'm walking on the street."

"I love your being so funny," she said.

That was another kind of love altogether, he thought. He didn't want to talk or hang up.

"See you there," she said. "Bye."

"Bye."

He put his phone back in his pocket. His stomach felt heavy, his feet felt heavy, his head felt heavy. He would meet her and he would listen to what she had to say although she had already said it. She could say it a thousand times and it would mean the same thing. And there was nothing he could
tell her.

The sadness went to his eyes. His vision blurred; he wiped the tears he felt wet against his cheeks. So many experiences so much time so much feeling together. But he was having his and she was having hers. It all had to do with his and her realities, he knew that.

A woman passed him on the street. Her reality was that she was going by this man in an overcoat and wearing a knit cap and was keeping on his side of the walk. She didn't look at him as he looked at her. He sought her face to see if any sadness was on it or happiness or dreams. Just for an instant. You can tell me everything about yourself, he thought. I will listen I won't judge. And he almost felt silly thinking that he loved her like he loved his eyes.

My eyes show me love as well as being my love, he thought. And he couldn't stop crying, the sadness of his future, of what was to be his future taken away from him. Where am I going? he asked and he meant in life not on what street or past what store or at what time. Where am I going? he asked and he knew he had no idea and no way to find out.

Maybe he didn't want to know. Going to Tony's at noon was enough.. He would figure it out from there.

He had quit thinking about her every second, every minute, then every hour. He had quit thinking about her every day even. He didn't know where that thinking had gone but it had kicked the bucket. He couldn't let it come back. If she doesn't want to be with me, then she doesn't want to be with me, he thought.

They were all on the planet anyway.

He hoped, really hoped, that rabbits didn't fall in love and break up and hop around miserable all day, unable to chew a sprig of grass. He hoped that cows didn't slobber on the dirt as they chewed it.

Love was something else to think about. But not now.

Sniffing, he felt better. Like he had cleared something out of his nose that had been there dusty.

We kill a lot of things, he thought, not just love. Love was easy to kill with words. But many things could not be killed with words. Like family. Or accidents. Dreams were killed in a moment. Pop, pop you're dead. Hope was killed like farting. So many things about life could be killed not just your body. Killing time was usually ok. Killing was sometimes glorified into be a swell thing, like a killer car. But killing feelings was hard. You had to plunge the knife in deep or get a big noisy gun and blast it in someone's face. But the most terrible thing to kill was not love. It was knowing about love, about how to get it and keep it or use it. No one could kill the knowledge of how to love and be loved. They could just kill the love, like killing a baby and not the ability to have a baby. I can love, he thought, I can love and I will love. That's what I should have told Susan. I'm okay because I can love. I will love.

The next person to pass him was in a hurry. Then a man passed and for no reason, he smiled and suddenly said, "Hello," as he walked on. When he glanced back, the man was glancing back. He nodded.

There you are, he thought.

He said hello to the next person who maybe didn't hear it. And to the next who also nodded. It was fun, like ringing a bell. Or like waking people up. As he walked, he listened to the hello's he said echo down the street. Hello, hello, hello, hello. It was fun, really. What if everyone did it? he asked. How nice that would be. Hello. Hello.. Why hello. Why hello. In all kinds of voices, different tones, everyone cheering themselves up. Speaking to these strangers was great fun. He turned back and looked. Yes, he could see his hellos down the street. And saying it improved his walk. He wasn't gloomy and dark. He wasn't sad. It was like stepping. Hello. Hello. Hello.

He could orchestrate it with his fingers if he wanted. Sing it loudly. Or whisper it. Or mouth it. Then he quit saying it and walked on silently.

The cold was rather obvious in how people dressed and in the redness of their cheeks. And in the clouds too.

When he got to Tony's he was early and chose a table by the window at the back of the room. He watched, waiting to wave at her as she entered. He knew how she would look, her brown hair long and soft and shiny and her red lipstick careful, her blue eyes looking for him. He knew how she would smell like spring flowers and he knew the movement of her body as she walked, like a parade. He always liked waiting and seeing her enter where they were meeting. He always had a coffee or a glass of wine waiting for her. He was waiting for her like the coffee and the wine and all he wanted was the same reaction that she had to them. If only she liked him like she liked the coffee. It pepped her up, flowed into her mouth and past her tongue into her throat like ambrosia. He wanted to be like the coffee.

He ordered coffee for her and for himself and laid the menu on the white tablecloth. The place was busy as it always was and he knew what he would order. But no, he wouldn't. He would think what he was hungry for. He hadn't eaten all morning.

What if she didn't show up?

What if I left? he asked. Quit being silly.

There she was, just coming in, her lips smiling and her eyes happy to see him like his were to see her. He needed to remember how she looked coming in. Like a photograph. She walked to the table and sat down.

"It's so cold," she said.

"Yes."

She looked him in the eye. "You look handsome," she said.

"You look beautiful," he said. They always said this to each other. It was part of the past. Even when he had stayed at her place, first thing no matter how they looked, they said it.

"I mean it," she said.

"I do, too."

"It's so good to see you. When we saw each other last and I left you had to most awful look on your face. You were so unhappy."

He smiled.

"And I just wanted to get away."

What? he thought. What was that? What did that mean? That he was sad and she wasn't? What did that mean?

"Anyway you look good now."

He wanted to ask her if she hadn't been sad, but he felt prideful. He chewed on his bottom lip.

"How's your work?"

"Good," he said. "Like always. Very good."

"It always is," she said. "That's one thing I've always admired about you."

He wanted to ask if she wanted to get together again. He did. It was everything to him. But he couldn't ask. He saw the answer on her face without her saying a word. It was in her smile. If she wanted to get together, she would be serious. That was all he wanted to ask. Nothing else mattered.

"I heard how upset you were," she said

So she was here to pity him?

"I missed being with you."

He knew no words now. Other than what he had thought earlier. "I still know how to find love," he said.

It startled her.

"I know how to find love and to love," he said.

She didn't like what he was saying. She was talking about their love not his ability to find love.

"Well, I do, too," she said, like it wasn't a nice thing to say.

"I will find it," he said..

"I'm sure you will,' she said. "I wish I could talk to you about it."

"Really?"

"You are still my best friend," she said.

She was right. They had been best friends and lovers. But all that had changed.

"So tell me about yourself," he said.

She laughed. "I've done a lot of shopping," she said. "And I've been seeing my friends."

He nodded.

"You feel better now don't you?"

"Yes, I do."

He wanted to ask her if she had met anyone else. He wanted to know who and what they did. He wanted to know how she felt about him.

"You should start dating. It's been a month. You'll feel better."

He had absolutely no idea what to say. She was like a stranger asking about his private life.

"You should," she said.

"I am," he said. But he wasn't.

"Who?" she asked. He could tell that she was upset.

"Myself," he said.

She laughed. "Then it's bound to be interesting. But I'm serious."

The waitress asked for their orders. He looked at the menu. If he was going to date someone different, he was going to eat something different. "I'll take the beans and franks," he said.

"You never eat that," she said.

He nodded, listened to her order, then he readjusted. "I'm glad you called," he said.

And he quit worrying about it.

Later, as he watched her walk away, down the street to her car, he waved at her back. "Bye," he said.

He repeated it. "Bye, bye."

Memories began to flood over him. Not just of her, but of himself as a boy. He couldn't even remember the names of some of his friends back then. He knew where they lived, what they had in their rooms, but he couldn't remember their names. He had a sense of connection with all of it. But the connection was circular, not linear. The past was not linear. He remembered lying in bed in his room and making important decisions. He couldn't even remember what they were. Who to ask for a date. He remembered that very well. The girls always went and he enjoyed dating more than anything.

But the past didn't interest him at the moment.

It was reality, and it was alive when he thought about it, but it mainly existed so he could think about what had happened to him and what he thought about it. It was a catalyst. Add in the past and things changed. Like garlic.

Part of my own reality is how I use my past, he thought. Not how it uses me. How I use it. The past is neutral.

Could this be true? Was the past neutral because it was over? Was it over? He believed the past was neutral and was not active. Of course he conjured feelings about it, of thing he missed or things that had happened that hurt him. But the past didn't have to be one way or another. How he used it, how he thought about it, determined what it was. His emotions were separate from the past, but he could use them to conjure up ideas of what had happened. It wasn't true. It was his emotions that were hungry.

My emotions are always hungry, he thought. Think about it. Anger made him go into the past and chew on things. Mainly hot things that upset him. What if he threw away his anger in the present and not let it dig into his past? Sex was more positive, digging just to enhance itself. Sadness seemed to be more focused on the moment. Nostalgia was different. Regret just gloried in the past. And fear—oh yes, fear used everything, past, present, future. It was a dilly of an emotion. Jealousy was another hurtful one. They flooded into his brain: pride, loneliness, shame, happiness.. They were like mosquitoes. Just sucking on him, using his every moment if he let them. He saw that he must use them, and not let them use him. That was strength.

So did his lunch upset him? Not if he looked at his feelings in isolation. Where was anger—when she said certain things. There was hurt, too. Yes. And there was pride listening. And shame. Goodness, he had just let the whole schoolyard out to play. Looking at each one, like a sword fight, he could parry and let them all go.

Where do you really want to live now? he thought. He had chosen the apartment because Susan liked it. She really had chosen it. He should find one of his own. He decided to walk to a different area of the city to see what it would be like to live there. This interested him.

He lived in the sixties, but he wanted to see the West Side. He had always thought it was different. Just ahead of him was Central Park. He entered it, the city around him like a dream and he crossed, the grass still green and the water in the pond rippling in the wind. When he reached the other side, he sat on a bench and looked up at the apartments across from him. He already lived in a highrise. He watched cabs hurrying along Central Park West, stopping and letting people out then letting others in. Everyone was caught in the act, arriving, going, waiting. Activity was everywhere. The doorman of the building in front of him was very busy, opening the door, going outside and helping certain rich looking women from taxis and lemos. The people all looked occupied.

An old man, well dressed and with a felt hat, walked up beside him. The man nodded and sat down. He carried a cane. Maybe he was waiting for someone.

Then he realized that the man wasn't waiting. He was alone. His loneliness was all over him, like a tan. It was loneliness dripping from his eyes and his mouth. It bore down on his shoulders and bent his head. It was in his desperate smile.

"Good morning," the man said.

"Hello," he said.

"This is a good place to sit and watch what's going on. I come here every morning."

"What do you see?" he asked the man.

It surprised him. "Well, yesterday there was a fire truck about two thirty in the afternoon. It didn't stay long. And a couple of days ago there was an accident. One car didn't stop at the light and hit another coming through the intersection. No one was hurt."

"A lot is going on," he said.

"Occasionally," the man said. He looked directly into Jim's eyes.

He was terribly sad.

"Why do you come here every day?" Jim asked.

"My wife. My wife died on November 21," he said. "I come here to get out of the apartment. We lived across the street for nineteen years."

"So you met death," Jim said.

"Or it met my wife. She was a wonderful woman. The best wife in the world. We were inseparable after I retired. I have a heart problem and I thought I would die first We both thought so. The doctor thought so. But that morning she got up and had a heart attack while she was preparing breakfast. We didn't know she had a heart problem. I don't know what to do with myself."

"This seems like a good thing to do," Jim said.

"I just sit here and think about her."

"Yes."

"I wish I could join her again."

Is that love? Jim thought. He didn't say it.

"I don't talk to many people but you looked kind of lost yourself."

"Yes, I am."

"Did someone die?"

"Part of me did."

"Yes, part of me did, too."

"Don't some animals grow new parts when something gets cut off?"

"I never thought about it," the man said.

"Just grow a new heart," Jim said.

"And how do I do that?"

"Take the seed and let it grow," Jim said.

"Yes."

Jim liked the advice. He decided to take it for

himself if the old man didn't like it. But the man was happy being so sad, that was clear. His emotions had married and needed to divorce. "Just take the seed and let it grow," Jim said.

The taxis kept flowing past. Jim nodded and got up. He waited for the light and walked across the street. He didn't want to live here. He didn't want to see the old man every day. He went down a narrow street toward Columbus Avenue, then Broadway. He went past.

He liked the little groceries, especially the ones with buffets. The restaurants had little outside tables.

The brownstones were mostly kept up. He could buy a walk through.

He had a funny idea. He'd like to live on his head and see things upside down. It was as useful as the old man sorrowing on the park bench. He supposed he had no family to speak of . He didn't speak of them.

And he asked himself about reality: could others see our reality better than we ourselves could? He thought not. His views of the old man had nothing to do with the man's reality, other than being someone sitting in the park beside him. He could not any more judge that man's reality than he could bring back his wife. The man felt his reality rather than knew it. That was his problem. Oh there I go again, Jim thought.

So did everyone have his own reality?

Yes. That was why he was seeking his own at this minute. He took a deep breath. Another one. Another one. Another one. He measured them. Another one. His life. His breath.

He decided to think about his learning, that is, his years in college and graduate school. He was what would be called well educated at good schools and making high grades. He had listened to thousands of lectures, read more books, and taken tests to prove it. He had continued reading and reading and listening and learning about specific topics: history, politics, literature.

And taken in a lump, what had it done to his reality? Much of it had focused it on the past. Or what it called the past. As if he didn't have enough of his own past, he had piled up the past of others, of countries, of the world. He had itemized it and kept in his closet, his apartment, his refrigerator, and mostly in his brain. This past he learned was actually the new past for him, just shoved in like chopped liver. He had been interested of course, but how had it affected his own reality?

It made me like everyone else, he thought. It certainly did. He could discuss all this past with multiple others like it was personal experience. But it wasn't.

It made him view who he was in a different light. His origin, his language, his achievements.

It made him more interested in much of the past than in what was going on right at the moment. His curiosity was often about other things, not in the mundane moment. His learning made much of his life mundane that really wasn't. It also made him dissatisfied with what he saw as his reality.

Hadn't what the old man learned made him more afraid of death? The world he was leaving; the world his wife had left? Didn't the old man see her as irreplaceable because of all they had learned together?

Everyone was shaped on the molecular level by their learning, he thought. By what others tell us about things we would never know otherwise. Did our minds need to be cluttered with so much? Did it interfere with our ability to use our emotions on their own? Did we need to be told what to know, what to feel and what to think? We did if we wanted to be alike. Otherwise, we didn't. And who we are was being replaced by what others wanted us to be.

It started from day one. His reality was a conditioned reality that he used to view living his life. This is what he wanted to see past, if even for one day. Was it even possible to know anything about ourselves on our own?

He decided he didn't want to live in this area no matter how beautiful certain parts of it were.

If a horse weren't kept in a barn, he thought, and weren't someone's property, how would he choose where to live? Would he sleep in the same place every night, under some tree? Would he have a sense of place? Surely he would. Rabbits had dens. Birds had nests. But how did they choose their dens and nests? Was it random choice?

Wasn't his? Of course.

Why not go up by Columbia and look, he thought? He'd have to take a bus, but at this point he would compromise. He got on the first bus going that way that he saw and sat at the back, the clatter amazingly loud.

He'd gone to Brown which was much smaller and confined in Providence. Columbia was a hub in the city to him. Its tentacles spread far.

He could see students and a professor riding in front of him. Most of them were reading; all were carrying packs. Their learning was imprinted on their faces.

My reality must be very flexible he thought, because I was one of these people in the past. He now was a business person, but he refused to think of that. Did his reality become one thing after another? Was it reflecting what was around him?

He thought not. Everybody was looking into the reflection of what they saw around them, but they were not that reflection. Otherwise, what a monstrous bore life would be.

Reality should not have a name he suddenly thought. Naming it took away its existence.

At the stop for Columbia the bus emptied and he got last in line to get off. Then he walked over and away from the school toward the river. It was quite different from where he lived and beautiful. It felt unfamiliar.

Years before he had gone to a party in one of these apartments.

His phone rang. He looked down. Susan. He accepted the call.

"Where are you?"

"I'm looking for a different apartment," he said.

"But I love your apartment. We took so much time to find it."

"But it was our apartment," he said. "I want to find one on my own."

"Okay." She was hurt.

"Why are you calling?" he asked.

"Because I saw you were upset at lunch. I feel so terrible that I made you unhappy."

"You aren't making me unhappy now," he said.

"Yes, I am."

"I'm making you unhappy. Isn't that why you are calling me?"

"I'm sad you are unhappy," she said.

"My god," he said,

"Well, I am."

"Okay. That's your choice."

"I bought you something on my way back to the office. I want to give it to you tonight."

He took a deep breath. "Tonight?"

"You can stop by if you want. I'm not doing anything else."

"Okay," he said.

"Try to feel better," she said.

"Yes," he said.

"Bye."

He realized that she wanted to get back together. Instantly he did feel better. Maybe they had only had an argument. Maybe she had only needed to be on her own for a while.

What would my life be like without her? he asked. Honestly he had never asked himself that. Not until this moment. He had assumed it would be sad and lonely like the old man's. Like he felt when she told him she wanted to break up. But he didn't feel that at this moment.

He felt like something beautiful had happened in his life. He had had to turn to himself and not anyone else. And that had been good no matter how hard it was.

Would he get together with her again? He had no idea. But right now, he wanted to be with himself, to let himself continue to think. He felt the floodgates open in his head. He was thinking on his own. It felt good. He couldn't do it at work or with Susan. He could only do it with his own company.

I appreciate being with myself, he thought. It was somewhat like loving his heart. He was loving his own company. He had not felt like that in years. Often he had hated being alone. He had used the cell phone to call others when he was in a cab or on a bus or walking down the street or when he was sitting watching tv or had nothing to do. Even when he was eating. I have neglected myself, he thought. I can enjoy my own company. How could I not have known that?

He had not listened to himself for years. And the trouble he had gone to, to avoid answering himself. That's what loneliness was. It was not answering the you that is trying to talk to yourself. Oh my god, he thought. He thanked himself for talking to himself. God bless you, he thought. Please realize that I do want to talk and know you. Why the better I know myself, the better I will know my reality and what I want and what I need to do. He felt a huge sense of relief. The next time I feel lonely I will know you have something to tell me, he told himself. And I will talk to you, too. I promise you. And he stopped. You are my own best friend, he thought. I love you. And his love for himself added to his love for his heart and his love for his eyes and his love for his love.

For a moment he felt like a great big drop of love. All inside and gooey and sweet like honey. He could taste it and feel it and if he wanted he could fall to his knees and thank god for it.

This is the part of reality that is like everyone else's, he thought. This is real.

He walked on, the trees flurrying, the clouds puffy, the light like tactile.

Well, no, he didn't want to live here, either. He decided to get back on the bus and just get off when he felt like it. If he couldn't find an apartment maybe an apartment could find him.

This bus was like the other with identical people on it. Even himself.

Some rode with their eyes closed, feeling the rhythm, or maybe being impatient. Several read newspapers. One was a nun in a habit. He wondered where she got it. The driver was as fat as the other and had a loud voice backing up the vocal system on the bus.

He rode a while with his eyes closed. Then he finally dozed, just a moment. He shook himself awake. Which was a good sign; it meant he wasn't worrying.

He decided to buy flowers for Susan just before he saw her tonight.

If he really did find a place he liked, he would rent it, he thought. He needed to.

A smaller place in an intimate building with people he knew going in and out. One with a grocery nearby and a cleaners and a playground. He lived in a high rise with a huge plaza and fountains and an endless underground parking garage. The view was like every other in New York. He'd be glad to move. And his lease was ending. Like it was supposed to all happen at the same time.

For one instant he blinked, thinking of returning to work the next morning. Then he forgot it.

Instead he decided to ask himself questions that he'd never thought of. Questions about himself that he needed to answer. Would he live his own life and not even find out important things he needed to know in order to make his decisions every day? Would he keep on living like his entire life was on a bus? One with no destination.

No. He would face himself.

First, he asked, what are you afraid of? He wanted to say nothing, but that was automatic. Then he wanted to say everything but that was automatic. I am afraid of....and he began to list things: of living alone; of not being loved; of not loving; of feeling useless; of missing out on life by not having what others have, of.... And these fears trailed off into an ant hole. These are the important fears, he thought: I am afraid of myself. I really am. I can be cruel to myself and make myself miserable. And I am afraid of god. I don't know why I should be but I am. He just left us with too many unanswered questions. If god is everything, why isn't he me? I don't want to be god, but if god is everything, am I part of him? Say I am. Let me know it. And why am I alive if I am going to die? Why throw death in? Why tell us? Just let it happen and no one knows, like clouds drifting by. Why do I have to know I'm going to die? Did I do something terrible in a past life or in this one? Please tell me what. I don't feel innocent..

He walked faster. I don't feel innocent at all and I don't feel guilty about anything I know about.

Was this insanity? Was fear insanity?

He believed in Christ, but was his belief enough and for those who didn't why make them suffer? He wouldn't make them suffer. Would Christ make them suffer? He didn't do that. Why make him afraid of even thinking about god? Like he'd get hit in the face if he didn't love. Well, he did love and although he didn't tell anyone he loved praying. The kind of praying that was thanking and thanking and loving. That was prayer. Why was god a jumble or was it only religion that was a jumble? No, everything was a jumble. Everything.

He didn't like his answer to that question but that

seemed to be it.

Next question: what did he want to get out of his life? Answer: was he supposed to get something? Or make something? Or see something? Or was the beauty of it that all of these things were true? Yes.

Next question: who had he hurt in his iife? He groaned. Put yourself on the list, he thought, and keep going. But he had hurt others mostly without trying. Just as Susan had him. Poor Susan, feeling responsible for his hurt. It wasn't hers.

Next question: How was he going to feel about his own life when he was dying? Answer: how could he answer this without dying? He had no idea. As long as God was alive, God was in control, not him. So what did his ideas of his life matter considering what God knew? Did God let pipsqueaks go on and on about their lives like they knew something? Please! God didn't have time for illusions.

These questions were unsettling. Important but unsettling. Go on, he told himself. Ask yourself.

Question: do you realize you are aging? Answer: That question didn't seem appropriate at the moment. He felt young, not old. It was for old people wasn't it? Of course he wasn't in high school or college or just learning to walk. Yes he was aging. Everyone and everything was. Time was a bitch. But so was water if you drowned in it. So forget time. Just wait until the final blink and bong! the clock stops.

Asking himself these questions he paid no attention to anything around him. He was lost in thought. Or what he called thought. It was his anyway. He got off the bus at the next stop and thought he'd find out where he was.

He stretched, once he got on the street. He'd passed this area before, in Chelsea, but hadn't liked it. He walked on, liking it better, looking at it from the street. It was expensive he thought. But he could find something here. The plus about living here was that he could start over. And it was far from Susan's.

So he had gone from miserable about her leaving to wanting to live far from her? Yes. For now.

Enough questions he told himself. He passed an old building with a vacancy sign for a one bedroom. That was perfect. He looked down the street at the myriad of stores. Yes a park was across the street. It had children. He stopped a minute and wrote down the number on the sign. The rent, expensive, was listed, too. He would look at it later in the week. But he wouldn't tell anyone he was moving until he'd signed a lease.

He decided he needed to go someplace quiet. Just ahead was a gallery he had heard of. It was open and he entered, quietly, taking his time looking at the works on display. He loved art of all kinds. As he looked, he felt that he could easily have become an artist of some kind.

Not that he liked what he was looking at, large cartoon type characters with huge price tags. He sat a moment in one of the futuristic chairs in the center of the room, allowing someone to take his time considering the works.

He had a sense that life was taking care of him. And it always had. The sense came from the quiet and the peacefulness of the place. There was a gallery and even a museum inside himself. Beautiful images he had seen and never forgotten. Beautiful people he knew or had passed by. And things that were beautiful because they were right. If he had wanted he could have sat in the chair for a year just seeing the beauty and the art from his own life. The term art was artificial. It wasn't learned—beauty was not learned. The beautiful was life—in nature, in thought, in people. Each inch of the sky was more beautiful than any painting. Every inch of a tree was, a flower was, a river was, etc. What he learned to call art was only a reflection of reality. If he could remember that reality meaning existence has a beauty then he could live in a kind of ecstasy. Even walking down the street, the glass, steel, wood, sidewalk, trees, cars, the people, the sky, the image of all was beautiful because it was real. It was this beauty, the beauty of the reality of existence that artists and writers were attempting to show. They were aware of their feelings more than others, maybe, but what they were doing was accessible to everyone.

"Can I assist you?" a very pretty dark hair young woman asked him.

"You are more beautiful than the paintings," he said.

She laughed. "Flattery will get you anywhere," she said. "Are you interested in any particular painting?"

"No thank you," he said, trying to be very kind in his voice so she wouldn't mind his speaking intimately.

He got up, without looking at the art and started toward the door.

"Come back to see us," she said, "We have new works go up every week."

"I will," he said, looking back and smiling.

He felt like he carried something with him when he left her. He brought it out onto the street and onto the sun which now was bright in the cold. It danced a moment, then left. He decided not to go back to his apartment before going to Susan's. He would just walk another two hours, and feel the freedom of it. Everyone walking around him felt it too, he thought. Just out in the air, walking, looking at whatever you wanted. Walking and looking. Such simple enjoyable things.

Remember that on your list, he told himself. Things we take for granted that are wonderful and we do every day without noticing. Showering. Walking. Exercising. Daydreaming. Thinking. Knowing. It was important, he thought, to think about what you know and don't. Knowing was very enjoyable. Sleeping. Using your voice. Your hands. Making motions. Delightful to just move your fingers and wrists and hands. Or his lips.

Make them into a smile. Pooch them out. Suck them in. Delightful.

He wondered how he ever could feel unhappy.

So he would have a drink before he went to Susan's. Just feel its warmth and taste. A beer or a scotch, he didn't care. Just something. A glass of wine. The taste of water. His tongue would be happy.

He entered a small bar just down the street. He would have to take a bus back to Susan's later. He sat at the bar next to a woman with a careful hairdo. He looked in the mirror at himself while the bartender took a moment. He was unshaven. But he recognized himself. People liked how he looked. Did he? He looked again. He pooched out his lips. He smiled. He liked it, too.

"You are so funny," the woman said. "Most people try never to show they are looking in the mirror. Here you are pooching out your lips and looking at yourself."

"I was making sure it was me," he said.

She laughed. "Is it you?"

"As far as I can tell," he said. "At least it's part of me."

"Well, it's a good part. You look very nice."

"So do you," he said.

"Thank you back."

"Why are you here at this time? It isn't dinner yet."

"I have somewhere to go later. I just wanted to get a drink."

"Me, too."

"You are drinking a vodka tonic," he said.

"Yes, I am."

"Why are you here?" he asked.

"I just got off of work next door," she said. "I'm an editor for a publishing company."

"You read a lot."

"Yes, I do. Do you?"

"More than I want to," he said.

"Me, too."

"Where are you from?" she asked.

"From Texas," he said. "You?"

"I'm a rare New Yorker," she said.

"Does that make you think of yourself differently?"

"What did you ask me?"

He repeated it.

"Why do you ask me that?"

"Do you have a sense of yourself outside of being a New Yorker?"

"In many ways," she said. "I'm a mother and wife."

"Outside of being a New York mother?"

"Absolutely. I'm many things outside of being born in New York. I know it's important. Do you think I could be from Texas like you?"

"No," he said.

"No? I think you are wrong."

"I'm generalizing I know," he said. "But I'm talking about how you view yourself. Wouldn't it be hard for you to think of yourself as a Texan? Not how someone else could view you."

"Yes, I agree. It's how I view myself. And you are a Texan. I couldn't imagine a New Yorker asking that question."

"Why are you getting a drink before going home?" he asked.

"That is personal," she said. But she smiled. "I like to relax after working all day. Just one drink. Then I go home and fix dinner for everybody."

"I think that's wonderful," he said.

"And why are you here?" she asked.

"I have no idea," he said. "Other than to talk to you."

"Then I'd better say something important," she

said.

"Everything you say is important," he said. "Because I don't know you and I won't ever see you again."

"I would think I wouldn't have anything to say because you don't know me," she said.

"No. Just the opposite. This is it. When I leave, it's over. We won't say another word to each other. What should we talk about?"

"If you put it like that, we'd better be honest."

"Yes."

"I come here because I'm lonely," she said. "I'm really not married and my children are grown. My husband is remarried to a much younger woman. I enjoy having a drink and not thinking of going home to an empty apartment."

"And I'm here because I'm waiting to go see my girlfriend who just broke up with me."

"I'm so sorry," she said

"I'm not," he said. "And I don't think you should be. You are looking at your life entirely from your past. Your kids are grown. Your husband is gone. That doesn't matter. You are in this bar right now. Your life is right now. The vodka isn't the best part of your life. Your enjoyment of it is and you can enjoy many many things if you let yourself."

"Oh," she said.

"Just listen to yourself and don't talk to yourself," he said. "Listen to what your heart is telling you."

"I know what you are saying is important," she said. "I know you are right."

"Your heart wants you to quit sticking pins in it."

"Oh, yes."

"You have everything," he said. "I know that."

"No one has ever told me that," she said.

"I'm telling you now. And I know. You have absolutely everything. Appreciate it."

She took a deep breath. "I've been waiting all my life for someone to tell me that."

"Don't forget it," he said.

"You have everything, too," she said.

"Yes, I do," he said.

"It doesn't matter if that silly woman broke up with you. Anyone can see that."

"And it doesn't matter if your husband left. He's an old goose."

"Yes, he is." Both of them laughed. "An old goose is right."

"I've got to go," he said.

"Thank you," she said. "Thank you for what you've told me."

"Just like I can see what's happy about you from the outside, you can see it from inside," he said.

"And you just tell that woman that there are many women in the world who'd love to have someone like you. Tell her you just met one of them."

He laughed. So did she. Then he gave her a hug, feeling her small shoulders and the silky blouse she wore. He kissed her cheeks, smelling her perfume. He felt that he loved her. "I love you," he whispered in her ear.

"I love you," she whispered back, smiling.

He got off the stool and walked out of the bar. Again the sky was golden and he was ten feet off the pavement. Glory, he thought. Glory. And he was so happy he had met her.

At six he knocked on Susan's door. She opened it, music in the background. "You're always prompt," she said

"We both are," he said. "What smells so good?

"Your favorites."

He sat on the sofa while she fixed him a drink. He leaned back on the cushion like he always did. The familiarity of the place seemed almost sinister.

"You looked terrible this morning," she said. "You

look so much better."

"I am," he said. And when he looked at her he thought of how unhappy he had been for the past month. He was more than unhappy.

"You were so unhappy," she said. "I was worried about you."

For the first time he didn't want to accuse her. To say that she had caused his problem. That he had been taken aback when she broke up with him. He had viewed it entirely as her fault. He realized it wasn't. "We should talk," he said.

"If you are ready," she said. "I'd like to clear the air. I want to tell you why I changed my mind."

"It isn't necessary," he said. "I think I had changed mine, too."

She was startled. "What did you say?"

"That I wasn't really aware of what I wanted. I was going along with what everyone else said was right. They told me how lucky I was. How good we looked together."

"We did," she said.

"I've thought it over,' he said. "I think I know why I was so unhappy when you ended us. I was too dependent on you. I see that now."

Her face was unhappy. She didn't speak.

"I hope you understand what I mean." He picked up a sofa pillow and began to squeeze it. He couldn't believe that he felt like he did. "I was afraid of being alone," he said.

"You can meet someone else easily," she said.

"As you can. But it has nothing to do with that. I really didn't want to be alone and I loved being with you. Now I realize that I can be with myself."

"Well, yes, you can. I've got everything ready. I'll put it on the table."

"I can help you."

"I have it," she said. "Just pour us a glass of

wine."

The meal was delicious as always. She was good at everything she did. He realized how beautiful she was as he sat across from her. He noticed every detail of her face. Like a work of art. "You're very beautiful," he said.

She smiled coldly. "I thought I'd be consoling you all evening," she said.

"Well, you are."

"I'm not sure I really understood you," she said. "You seem entirely different."

"I didn't understand myself," he said. "Have you ever thought about how wonderful life is?"

"How can you say that now?" she said. When she looked at him, she seemed to have tears in her eyes.

"What do you want?" he asked her.

"I want...I want...us to be friends. I told you."

"Well, we are." It seemed like a little dumpling of a thing to be. "I'm your friend," he said.

She began to cry. "I don't know what happened to us," she said.

He put his arms around her and held her as she cried. He stroked her hair, feeling how soft it was. He kissed it, smelling the perfume of her shampoo.

When she sat up, she said nothing.

"Everything's okay," he said.

She nodded. A few minutes later, he stood up and said he had to go. She got up, too. She walked him to the door.

He leaned down and kissed her.

Then he left.

As he walked down the street to his apartment not far away, he did not know what had happened. He thought that maybe she wanted to be together again.

It was night and still cold. He would go inside his apartment and turn up the heat, then play some music He would try not to think about her. For weeks he had been so unhappy there. Now, his place seemed a refuge.

He liked it. It was very comfortable with everything he enjoyed.

In fact, he felt that he had had a wonderful day. Just trying to think of who he was and what it meant to be himself. He wished he could tell her about it. He wished that he could tell everybody. Everybody in the world had so much to tell about themselves.

On *Birdsong*

"**An eye for detail at once sharp and tender**" *Punch.*

"**It's beautifully done...I admire the simplicity and naturalness of the writing...**" Anne Tyler (Pulitzer Prize winner)

"**It's on a list I keep in mind, of novels that have startled me into recognizing that it is the work that matters. I've taught *Birdsong* several times...**" Thomas Williams (National Book Award winner)

"**What a delight even if a difficult delight! It must have been to write it!**" Gwendolyn Brooks (Pulitzer Prize winner)

"**Such a beautiful moving book!**" Wallace Fowlie (National Book Award Winner)

"**I am very impressed by the precision of language and controlled, emotional understanding in** Birdsong." James Alan Mcpherson (Pulitzer Prize winner)

"**I loved it all the Way Through.**" Christopher Isherwood (Author of *Berlin Stories*)

"***Birdsong* is a small masterpiece of emotional precision, moving, simple, beautifully written.**" John Clellon Holmes (author of *Go*)

"**I was drawn into the pages and saw quite soon that the beauty of it was in the way you let the material just be itself.**" Elizabeth Hardwick, Publisher, *New York*

"The novel is a masterpiece of simple beauty...you cannot put *Birdsong* down." *El Paso Times*

A poignant reenactment of a rite of passage, fragile and joyous as the title." *Library Journal*

"Touching, deceptively simple...Mr. White captures precisely the essence of small realities, the reality of dreams." *Sunday Telegraph*

"This simple tale is engrossing and powerful; it became, for me, a kind of searchlight by which I could view again much of the joy and idealism and tedium and pain and wonder of my own youth." James Leo Herlihy (author of *Midnight Cowboy*)

"White's marvelous idiom renders the world of this small Texas town with uncanny accuracy and tender affection...His characters glow with life." Sylvan Karchmer

"We have from the first page that sure sign of a talent for fiction, the power to make vitality and a sense of real life arise between the lines." *Dallas Morning News*

"*Birdsong* is fine, very real, very moving. It seems a cannon should go off after a work of such patience and skill." Joanne Leedom Ackerman (author of *A Dark Path to the River)*

"I read *Birdsong* very slowly, but I didn't want it to end. I love (not like) *Birdsong*. People need books like that." Susan Fromberg Schaeffer

On *The Persian Oven*

"White, who formerly ran the USC writing program, has a wonderful ear for dialogue and a terrific writer's eye for what is essential." *Publisher's Weekly*.

"*The Persian Oven* is highly successful...his conventions make him a writer who goes his own way." *Times Literary Supplement* (*London Times*)

On *Observations Without Daddy*

"*Observations Without Daddy* is a crystalline portrait, a precise rendering of the life of a thoughtful and independent boy growing up in West Texas....White's memoir is certainly satisfying, a small triumph I readily recommend. The voice is strong, consistent, perceptive, the details evocative, the reflections poignant." *American Book Review*

"I enjoyed the same quality in *Birdsong*, the 'wide-eyed' completely unprejudiced estimate of the people surrounding him...it all reads so well and authentic." Ruth Jhabvala (Booker Prize, Academy Award winner)

On *I Am Everyone I Meet*

"The people White talks to, because it is Los Angeles, come from all over the world. This makes the vignettes even more fascinating." *Los Angeles Times*

On White's writing:

"The simplicity of White's writing draws one to it as graphite to a magnet*." El Paso Times*

"White has the voice of a true writer in the Chekhovian tradition, a voice that betrays no interest whatever in its own brilliance: all of the considerable light it sheds is focused upon the unremarkable human beings who are the stuff of his books, never shining back upon the author. This is the work of a man who clearly understands, as few novelists do, that the business of literature is mankind."
James Leo Herlihy (author of *Midnight Cowboy*)

"His characters glow with life." *South Central MLA Bulletin*

"It is in the writing that White is most impressive… His poet's eye for the evocative detail and his short story discipline of densely freighted textures have provided a method." *San Antonio ExpressNews*

Made in the USA
Middletown, DE
11 October 2020